T0198827

Worthwanderer

At the set time, Unnarangnorom, the Worthwanderer, removed Sokhen and Sokhit from Kingsworth to the Realm of Briskfalls.

Sokhen and Sokhit

Where the two vile Kings ecstasy-spiraled
downward until they came before the Monnarok.

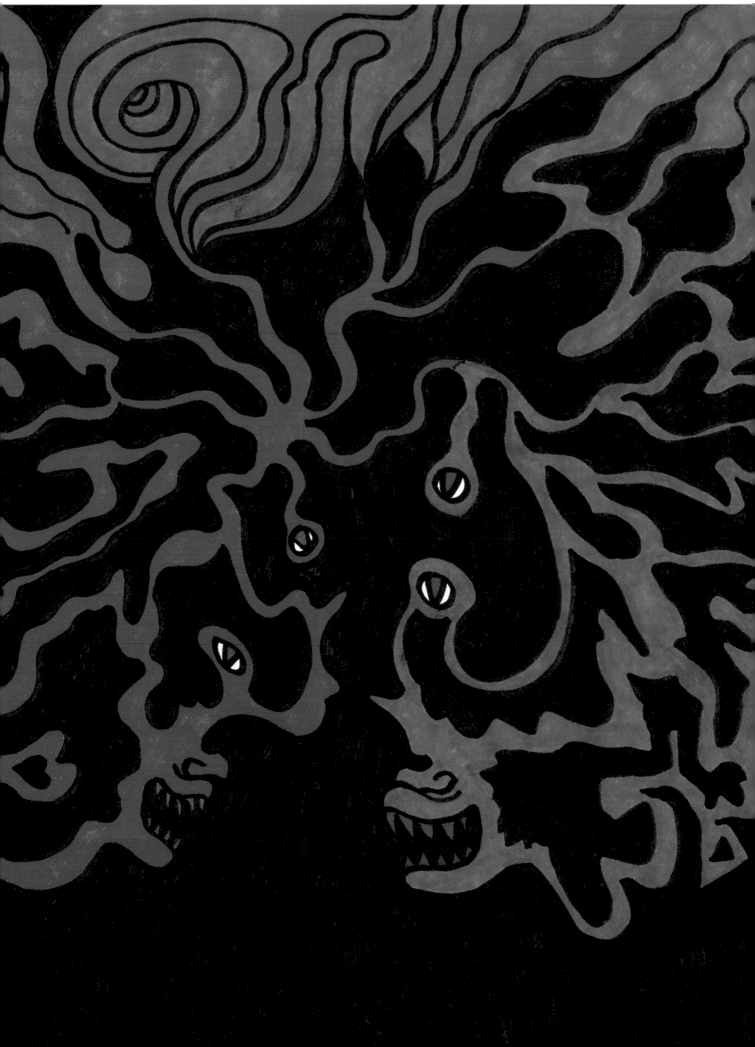

Clask

And they made a covenant
with the Squalid Squad.

Zetel

So the Monnarok placed the
men's iniquity upon themselves.

Squalid Squad

Without delay, Sokhen and Sokhit worked
valiantly as Knightkings of the Momentary
Allegiance for their new Masters.